I0624798

The Transition of a Poet

by

Tamara Hamilton

Forever Inspired Publishing

The Transition of a Poet

Printed by Lulu Press Inc., in the United States of America
First printing, August 2020

ISBN 978-0-578-72937-4 (paperback)

Published by Forever Inspired Publishing
PO Box 66442
Virginia Beach, VA 23466

9780578729374

The Transition of a Poet

The Essence Of Me

The essence of me is still there
Though sometimes it seems
hazy like a summer afternoon
Maybe that is what's important
Not necessary the physical form
Who you are. Being..
This takes away a bit of every
part of me
I am not what I used to be
With that, it is trying to
change my spirit
Trying
Not allowing it to get to the best
part of me
The essence of me
Is still there
It won't ever change

Trying To Fly

I want to run so far away from what you are giving
What you have taken
My heart is still breaking
 And I need the glue that only you can seal.
What you say you feel
For me
Is it really real? Foolish, fool
Weak, weakness
Is what I feel…
I don't want to crash and burn
I was flying when I was with you
Then hovering when you took the wind from my wings
Confusion
Is what I have in my mind
Love
Is what I have in my heart
Hesitation
Is what is badged on my soul
Again my heart is still breaking
And I need the glue that you have to seal
Me.
Only you can heal, I want this to be real
I know I have to fly
But only with you by my side

What You Do

The aura and essence of the love I have for you cannot
be explained
It pulls me and draws me to create
with you
Everything you do for me
It is more than physical
My spiritual growth depends on it
The elements of you make me
You allow me to be free
You have been with me so long I
couldn't imagine responding living
without you there
There have been times I fell back
from you but you always been where
you needed to be
You uplift me
You never disappoint me
What you give me is me
Music

Give

What do you want me to do?
What I do, I can't do anymore
Cause right now my heart, my
feelings, my soul should mean
more to you
(Should be above anyone else)
Give me a reason to make me stay
Not stay away
Giving..I give
You don't give enough
You can't when you want to make
another happy
You belong to me
You belong to me in every way
I should be first with you...
I gave you me
I put you where you should be
At the beginning, at the start,
on top, in front of everyone
I did that when my body was in
a space it had never been
I made my decision then
So give me a reason to make me stay
Not stay away
Give me the one thing you have a hard time giving
If you can't, If you can't
I can't stay

Lost

I lost me somewhere in between the cheating, the lies,
the distrust, the deception,
The heartache, the sleepless nights, the fights.
The love.
Don't know how to get it all back.
Been searching but maybe I am looking in all the wrong
places.
Been fighting but maybe I am fighting for the wrong
things.
This path I have chosen is more than I expected.
But what isn't in life?
Gave what I shouldn't
Receive what I didn't want
I replaced what was sacred to me with the profane and
unkempt
Nirvana

Loving

Love is not hard. We make love hard. Loving is simple.
Not complex.
We expect it to be one way.
And we..
We don't appreciate what is given.
We make it hard.
Life. Our experiences make it hard.
It is so hard to love.
It is so easy to love for some.
But the hurt is hard.

Him and Them

Persecution of a life
Of his life.
The means to control
The need to express the evilness that you harbor within.
You are not his master
Nor is he your slave.
Why the oppression so?
You are afraid of him.

Him..
I am afraid for you.
I am afraid for you all the time.
Because the advantage is take all the time.
And the focus is on hurting, anger is constant.
Why the hate for a man that is no different from besides color?
Why despise a man that has done nothing to you?
You are afraid of him.
Whether he knows it or not he is blessed to be who he is.
He is defining, magical, strong and can continue to be legendary.
You are in awe of that.
You are threatened by him.
You are always afraid.

Sailing

Peace is where I want to be with you. There you and I
can be free.
Pain is the island that we are on and I am trying to sail
away.
Do you want to sail away with me?
Let go of all that has your mind and heart
All that is holding you hostage.
Your armor has become rusted and tainted.
And mines is weighting me down
Want to shed it before it brings us down and we can't
come back up.
We can't breathe.
Want to feel the breeze of calmness in our spirit and
warmth of your unequivocal love.
Come sail with me

Intentions

I feel your false intentions
I see your wicked dimensions
You show me how you are in all different types of
conditions
This has no honorable mentions
Just renditions of the same role you so adeptly play.
I put aside the conventions.
My pride was at your feet
Persistently
Consistently
I sow, you reap
Until I fall so deep
I was sleep, my mind weak
And soul caught
This love, choice for naught
Choices was choosing
I was losing something I never really had
I can't help but be sad because I was there
And maybe you were too
On the inside I knew
It never really was that meant to be shit
I made myself not believe it
So now I got to deal and move
And choose what it needs to be
How it is ain't always what you want to see it to be
Giving it time and space
To replace all the anxiety of a love misplaced

Intro/Interlude

Here I am before you
Want to get to know you
Know me
All the things I dream, it never ceases to amaze me
All the things I've seen never seems
to dissuade me
Where my heart is
What my soul shows
It is slicker than SoulGlo
And hopefully it will make you as high as the antidote on
the night show
This is the Intro
to me

My Creation

The seeds of your creation, your garden
Should grow bountiful
In the meaning of things
She is what I want to be
He is what I hope to be
They are the best of me
I gladly give them that

Necessary

Thinking about the realities of my life
Not breaking rules but breaking sleep
Allowing the negative, the frivolous
to influence me
I don't want these words to sound as
jumbled as my mind is (be)
So let me focus on the need and the necessities of
being me
I need love, total adoration and respect
Right at this moment that is a necessity that will not be
circumspect
Being brave in a world of weak souls is what I show but
am slow to react when needed
Am I needed, a necessity to you?
You can get by with the negative and frivolous goals and
bullshit ambition you have within you
But I can not
There is more to the world than pussy, drink, being lit
I know it now but you won't know it until you are bend to
breaking
Is a better man in the making?
Don't know but a better woman is
Will not continue to give up what is sacred for the sake
of it
That is your life
What you care to know
What is important to you so peace my nigga
Exalted became the goal
It became the need
The necessity so let's get ready, set, go

Excuse Me

Well excuse me if I excuse myself
from your excuses
Your abuses
And you being obtuse
To what I see and what you do
I refuse to get use to
the way we are living
No matter how my brain relays the truth
Yet and still I invite you back
No matter how my mind reacts to your actions
It would continue to be this way if you continue to have
your way
But I would rule the day as I rule my soul
My mind tells me that it is something better if I let it
My soul tells me that it is low but not depleted
I will give to yours if you give to it first
Cuz you're needs to be mended as mines needs to be
attended to
I am looking toward the light
Looking towards God and what she says do is be there
with you
And I will. Just differently.
Sufficiently. Assuringly. For you

I Believed

I believed in you for years
I believed in us
I believed that we were better than what we portrayed
We are past the cusp
Of the downcast tears and falls

The pitfalls,
I been through it all and I can't seem to resolve my fears
Trying to absolve you from the pressure
But can't get past the treasure I thought I was
Wished I was to you
I won't ever cause this is greater
Than what I can do

The Sun

The sun...
I want to touch it
I do sometimes
I feel it all time..
The warmth, the light
It fills me
But it blinds me too
Wear shades, you say
I cannot
I don't want too
Not supposed to
The extra energy, influence, is only when I am not ready
Confusion
Not discontent
That is not what this is about
Just close my eyes and open myself to it
Recharge with it
Be into what I am because of it

Freedom

Freedom.
It isn't all in the mind
but that is where it starts
My eyes saw open fields far away,
uninhibited truths in the distance
Fears, doubts holding me back and holding me close
It won't allow me to be contained any longer
Freedom beckoned my spirit
and I finally decided to let it in my reality
My body followed, as my soul led the way towards
Freedom

The Children

Children are life forces
Don't be putting out their fire with your bullshit
Build it increase it so the gods can see it from wherever
they are and pay homage to you

But you don't know how to do that do you? Being you
are so fucked up.

At one point it was not your fault but on this day know it
is. You make the choices and you can always make the
choice to be better.

Heal up

Beneath all the fun, the glamour (and that ain't nothing
but what is says it is), the drinks, the clothes is a person
who.....
What?

Be better. Growth.

Listen

(You don't listen to me)
I got to fight to get my voice heard
But right now do you hear the silence?
That is my voice
My opinion
My views
Me. Invisible.

Imperfect Perfection

Perfection is what I thought we had when I saw your
eyes sparkle with
the secret of unknown delights
But in this light that is blinding my soul, I am not so sure
I adore your touch,
endure your actions until it can go no more
Say 'No more' to me and I will cease the heart play,
the whispered words that I can't get you to stay..
in this place of fulfillment and inbounded design
But every time I get drunk off your passion as if it was
wine
Time, oh, it seems to stand still until it moves to the
unforeseen
and I can't see..you anymore in this imperfect dream

The Plan

You are feeling me,
Being me,
In this world
Where robots rule.
Be so consumed,
by the bigotry and the unjust
I just wish
things were different.
And they could be
Not ever this monotony and this battle that I have within
I pretend it is all great
But I am about to clean the slate
Cause I must
The Gods keep showing me
Providing me with these tools
So I won't lose

Know..
The plan never was the plan
It was the excuse
For the resistance and still existence

For those
They are stuck in a warp of falseness and lashes
I feel twenty lashes each time I fall prey to mediocrity
The dependence of likes...
Of you liking me
Wanting me
These emotions belong within each other
To each other
To given to the lost souls that are have already let go
Let go then let go

It is bottled in
It is a deadly sin to be this contained
I maintain the devotion to the notion of greatness
No fake-ness, falsity
Just embracing our creativity
Breaking chains and rules
Throwing holy water on these fools
Til they lay smoldering at our feet

FIX

Right from the start
This drug you got me in is not for the light heart
It is gathered and consumed with fear
With every tear I reveal,
my inner essence.
With every blow it rips away my glow
But I don't care
I am sliding on this high,
feeling no remorse
This course is dedicated to our intercourse, the sex
Which is next
Initially I am perplexed to why this has to be this way
But again after that first shot
all my reluctance is swept away.
Stay. Until the next time I feel low

Enter, On Course

Nerves is what will on edge when we put to bed our
ideals and ourselves.
I choose to feel, the greatness and circumference of all
you have to give.
Put my body in motion as my soul shows it devotion to
your mass appeal.
You are a big deal.
So real when you come to my escape..
from your lesser woes.
My toes clinch and my ocean wrench you into my oasis
is what this moment shows

Audience and Reviews

This niche that we are in is elusive
Differences make us exclusive
Unattainable not debatable
The way we are born to be
Defining all odds with our breathe
And every beat of heart, a staccato
I just heard someone yell Bravo!
Or whispered?
Fears and hate simmered
until it overflows
And we go into overload
feeling, believing and knowing what we are denied.
This won't be held inside.
Forces will be known and our actions will be guided

These Emotions

These emotions,
I'm coping
with how I feel about you.
I get open
for anything you do.
A smile, one kiss
I can't resist
I can't shake
Can't break this hold
This hole... doesn't even end
Like Alice, but this ain't no Wonderland
Rejection? Connection? Confusion...
Feeling the illusion
I put myself in
No substance
Abruptness needs to set in
Cause I am emotionally involved

A Quiet Death

A quiet death
I don't need someone to uplift and move me, let all this
Rescind in a quiet death
The love, the energy that you supposedly feel
Let it resound in a quiet death
The nights we felt like them Caribbean days
Reside in a quiet death
Of all the medically remorseful things that made my
heart
I am so resourceful that I will use the lessons
Rightfully,
I wanted the spirit of us to flow gradually, graciously
toward the earth
and towards the skies
Bury all this love, feelings, longing but also disperse in
the clouds

Good To Be (Reservations)

It feels good to be who you are…
with no reservations,
Come sit at my table and tell me what makes you
a star.
One that is special when it shines bright.
No matter the light,
Day or night I can get addicted to show you put on.
Cause you have always been gifted
Promise you will never hold back,
continue to be true to all you were to meant to do.
There is always room for you in the sky…

A shooting star that flies.

Earth and Seeds...Urgencies

You force your energies on me

You affect your energies on me
I am well aware of your tendencies of not believing
in what we
as in me, perceives this to be
I get anxious with equations that don't add up
I keep trying to be fed up
But I am full up with your body in my mines
My mind...
Filled up with the memories or is it fantasies? Of
us
It is just me?
Saying yes it is you.
It's been you all the time
Go slow...
While I turn down the r and b song flow in my head
While giving you head
I am headed for defeat
As we are down on these sheets
I meet you until I can't feel my heart beat
Knowing that not one time yours made a sound
Empty soul...profound

Reflecting US

Showing is knowing
Knowing is showing
yourself that the world is bigger than the object at
the tip of your fingers
When anger, makes you a stranger
to reality
We are in danger of becoming a droid with no
autonomy
We govern our desires
Hide behind pain
Showing no shame
I shake my head at the quest for fame

They don't see how beautiful they are!
But that is the purpose
To make us feel nervous
And slighted by what others have
Gentrifying cultures
Social vultures
Taking everything that means something til it is the
mass of dead bodies and gray areas
No more color and light where they bury ya
Just shells......
And noise. Sounding like radio frequencies
Listen!
Don't mean to offend
Or to upend your 'beliefs'
But feeling friction
This dictation of my dissertation
Giving you the benefit of my benediction
of growth
Alienating myself from all that outside noise.........!

Turning down the volume on the source
Sounding staticky and
It is clouding my thoughts.
Bracingly I pull my wroughts to the front of this
altar
Faltering is possible but not an option
But these are my steps as I move towards
adoption of greatness and light
With all my might I resisted this thing you called
'LIFE'.
It is more than just breathing, believing and living
someone else's ideals
Frills and thrills on your carousel wheel

Memoirs of Love

Remembering what was golden
Molding my thoughts around my love memories of
you and us
It's got me glowing
Slowing down and taking into account now, all my
visions that were locked away.
Just behind my eyelids,
I see in mid -motion,
you kissing and holding me
It glimmers and glistens
I am missing you..
All your affection & attention
And all your grumpy ways.
Oh I loved your displays
The days go into nights
I recite but don't have to ever rewrite
Cause I had the real thing
Dreams are recorded my temporal lobe
and imprinted on my soul

Awaken to Greatness

I am on my way to something
Where time matters not
I am on my way to something
Where I feel overstanding is the plot
I am on my way to something
And it won't even stop
Being prolific
This craft, I am gifted (with)
I won't miss this
Opportunity to rock
I am on my way to something
As the moon moves towards to stars
I recite these bars
For you and I
Full of gratitude and my
Heart races as the day ends
The way my life contends
You's a fool if I allow men -tion of your fakeness
Dictate this
My actions
Satisfaction is the caption
This really is full blown
Awakeness is the stake in this
I am on my way to something
And it is Greatness
I am taking my place and making
Sure I don't miss a moment
I am on my way to something
And when I reach it, I'm going to own it
Being prolific
Gifted
I am on my way to Greatness

www.ingramcontent.com/pod-product-compliance
Lightning Source LLC
Chambersburg PA
CBHW030544200626
46812CB00020BA/1807